Richard Scarry's
BEST BALLOON
RIDE EVER!

A GOLDEN BOOK • NEW YORK
Golden Books Publishing Company, Inc., Racine, Wisconsin 53404

Harry Hyena, Benny Baboon, and Wolfgang Wolf
—the Three Beggars—are fishing for something to eat.

"I'm SO hungry!" says Harry.

"All we have caught today is an old boot and a
tire," adds Benny.

"We never catch *anything* to eat!" says Wolfgang
with a groan.

Meanwhile, in Busytown, there is much excitement. Everyone has come to watch Rudolf von Flugel take off in a balloon.

Huckle and Lowly think the balloon is very interesting.

"Would you boys like to climb aboard for a minute?" asks Rudolf.

The boys climb in and look at all of Rudolf's equipment.

There is a compass, a map, and some bags of sand.

"Rudolf," Lowly asks, "don't you want to take a picnic with you?"

"How silly I am!" Rudolf replies. "I knew I had forgotten something. I will be right back!"

Rudolf jumps out of the basket.

Without Rudolf, the
basket is lighter.
    Suddenly the balloon
begins to rise.

"Mr. von Flugel! Help!"
shouts Huckle.

Father Cat tries to grab the basket, but it is too late. Soon the balloon is high in the sky above Busytown!

"This is terrible!" says Huckle. "How will we ever get down?"

"Don't worry," says Lowly. "We will manage somehow."

The balloon flies over the countryside. There is Farmer Beanstalk's farm. There are the woods. Soon they are over Busytown Beach. Below they can see everyone running after them.

The balloon sails out over the water.

It seems to be getting
tired of flying. It starts
to come down.

"Lowly, we're going to crash into the water!"
Huckle says.
"Throw out a bag of sand!" Lowly orders.

Just before it touches the waves, the balloon climbs into the air again. Oooof!

The wind pushes the balloon
to the opposite shore, just where
the Three Beggars are fishing.

Harry Hyena raises his fishing pole to cast his
line. "This is my last try to catch something to eat!"
he says with a sigh.

But instead of coming down, Harry's pole begins to rise. His line has caught the balloon. "Help! Help!" he cries.

Benny and Wolfgang grab Harry. They hold him with all their might.

The balloon stops traveling.

"Don't let go!" shouts Lowly.

Lowly pulls the rip cord, opening the top of the balloon. The balloon deflates, and the basket bounces softly onto the beach.

SPLASH! The Three Beggars tumble backward into the water.

Sergeant Murphy, Rudolf, and Father Cat speed across the water in a motorboat.

"Thank goodness you boys aren't hurt!"
says Father Cat.
"You are the best balloonists ever!"
praises Rudolf.

"And you are the best fishermen!" Sergeant Murphy tells the Three Beggars.

"I suppose so," replies Harry Hyena, "but we are also the hungriest! We never catch anything to EAT!"

Rudolf reaches into the motorboat and pulls out a picnic basket. "This time I remembered to bring the picnic!" he says, handing the basket to Harry, Benny, and Wolfgang.

The Three Beggars all agree that this is their best—and their biggest—catch ever!